To Cathy

MW01126147

Daniel

KINGS OF
KORRUPTION
novel

Enjoy!

by

GERI GLENN

Geri

Glenn ♥

A Kings of Korruption MC Novel
Book Two-Point-Five
By
Geri Glenn

©Geri Glenn, 2016

Daniel is a work of fiction. All characters, organizations and events portrayed in this novel are either products of the author's imagination or used fictitiously.

This ebook is licensed for the personal enjoyment of the reader. It is the copyrighted property of the author and may not be reproduced, copied or distributed for commercial or non-commercial purposes.

Cover Art
Wicked by Design

Editing
ACS Media

Formatting
Tracey Jane Jackson

ISBN-13: 978-1539064848
ISBN-10: 1539064840

This story was originally written for the OAMC Anthology that went to benefit Project Semicolon. An incredible organization, and a cause near and dear to my own heart. Mental health is so very important. This book is for anyone who ever felt alone.

http://www.projectsemicolon.org

Gabby

"**W**hat did you just say?" I ask, feeling like I've just been punched in the stomach.

The officer smirks and shakes his head. "Look sweet-heart, I know you're worried about your brother, but the truth is, punks like him go missing every day. He'll turn up a couple of weeks from now in some crack house, strung out and looking for his next hit. We don't have time for that shit. I'll file the paperwork, but I doubt we'll find him."

With every word he speaks, my heart pounds faster and my anger grows. My nineteen-year-old brother hasn't been home in two days and I know something is wrong. Derrick wouldn't do that. He wouldn't just leave me all alone like that. I don't know what to do. Going to the police is what you're supposed to do when someone you love goes missing. Now this cop is telling me that they don't have the time "for that shit"?

I clench my fists, take a deep breath, and try to calm my racing thoughts but it's no use. Worry and fear for my brother, combined with the anger I feel at this asshole cop, bubble up to the surface and overflow.

"Are you fucking kidding me right now?" I shriek, as I jump to my feet. "My little brother is *missing*! You're the *police*! And you're telling me you don't have time for this shit?"

He leans back in his chair and cocks an eyebrow at me. "I'm gonna have to ask you to sit down, Miss Monroe."

I stare at him in disbelief. His eyes bore into mine, daring me to argue. Just seeing that look on his face allows the hopelessness I feel to overwhelm me. My breaths come in short and shallow pants. I take a deep breath in an attempt to slow it down and collect my thoughts.

"I said sit *down*."

My eyes widen. I can barely contain the anger in my shaking voice. "I want to talk to someone else."

He chuckles humourlessly. "Sorry, honey. I'm the best you're gonna get. Now sit down and let's fill out the paperwork. It's almost lunchtime and I have a burger with my name on it waiting down at the diner."

I can't even look at this guy. This was a waste of time. Turning, I wrench open the door and storm from the room, retracing my steps to find the exit. My face heats with rage and I feel murderous. Through the haze of my anger I see several people milling about, both in and out of uniform, as I pass. Behind me I can hear the cop running after me, angrily calling my name.

"Miss Monroe! Miss Monroe!" I keep storming, the heavy door to the lobby now in sight. "Miss Monroe! Stop right there!"

Narrowing my eyes, I freeze and slowly turn to face him. His face is reddened and a thin sheen of sweat has formed on his brow below his receding hairline. He opens his mouth to speak but I throw up my hand effectively cutting him off before he even gets started.

"Forget it! You're a fucking prick. I'll find my brother myself! I don't know how I'm gonna do that, but I refuse to waste my time on a report that you likely won't even file. Now, fuck you very much but I need to get out there and find my brother!"

With those parting words out of my mouth, I spin around intending to continue my storm out of the building but come face-to-chest with an officer wearing dress pants and a dark grey button-down shirt. Just as I'm about to slam into him, he raises his hands to my shoulders and stops me. He's tall. Very tall.

I lift my eyes, pissed that he's trying to stop me. I open my mouth to argue, but pause when I see him glaring over my shoulder. "What's going on here, Frank?"

I continue to stare up at his chin, unsure of what to do next, when I hear from behind me, "Miss Monroe here wanted to report a missing person. I was trying to help her do that when she went crazy and stormed out."

The man's chin tips down and I find myself looking into the most beautiful pair of green eyes I've ever seen. "Is that true Ma'am?"

I stare at him another beat before realizing that he just asked me a question. Clearing my throat, I think back to what has just been said and I snap out of my daze. I am instantly furious all over again.

Pulling back, I slam my fists onto my hips and turn my body so that I can see both officers. "No it is not!" I declare. "I came in to get help finding my brother, and this guy," I jab my thumb in the direction of Officer Asshole, "said he was likely strung out in a crack house and that he didn't have time for this shit." I look back to the concerned officer. "I just want to find my brother. I don't have time to waste at a police station if nobody is going to help me."

He stares at me while I tell my story, his jaw clenched tightly as I speak. When I am done his eyes swing to the other officer. "Frank, I'm reporting this."

Frank rolls his eyes. "Whatever, man. The kid she's looking for is a punk. He's messed up with the Crips. There's no way in hell we're gonna find him."

The well-dressed officer's body is visibly tight and I can feel the anger coming off him in waves so I'm surprised when his eyes focus on me with a softness that makes my belly flutter. "Ma'am, please. Let me work on this with you. Of course we will do everything we can to find your brother."

I hear Officer Asshole scoff at his co-worker's words but I'm too busy staring up at this beautiful policeman who is finally offering me some hope. My eyes wide and filling with tears of gratitude, I nod slowly. He gently takes my elbow and leads me past the indignant cop and right back to the room I just left.

"Have a seat. I'll be back in just a few minutes."

I nod at him wordlessly and slide back down into my still-warm seat. He stares at me for a moment before returning my nod and walking back out into the hallway, closing the door behind him.

My mind is spinning. My anger at that jerk cop has my body shaking with adrenaline, but now that I know this new guy is going to help me, I am filled with relief. I just want to find Derrick. He's all I have left since Mom moved away to live with her new husband, who Derrick and I hate with a passion.

Just then, a loud smash from out in the hallway makes me jump in my seat. This is quickly followed by angry shouts. I can't make out the words from behind the closed door, but I do recognize the voice of Officer Asshole. The shouts are quickly followed by a low, gruff mumble and then silence.

I sit quietly, ears straining to hear what comes next, but there's nothing. A few seconds later, the door opens and in walks the new cop. "Alright, Miss Monroe. Let's get working on finding your brother."

Daniel

My blood is still boiling as I sit down across from her. Fucking Frank. How that guy ever became a cop is a goddamn mystery to me. He is one of the laziest assholes I've ever met. In fact, I have no clue what he even does around here. I am done with his bullshit. I'm taking this right to the Chief when I'm through with Miss Monroe. He can't treat people like this, and he's been getting away with it for far too long.

Taking a deep breath, I shove all thoughts of Frank Johnston out of my mind and focus on the girl across from me. It's not hard to do. She's beautiful and…different. Her hair is long and black, the curls cascading halfway down her back. She has a large white flower tucked just above her ear that matches the flowered dress she's wearing. Her blue eyes are made up dramatically with heavy eyeliner and smokey lids, and her lips are a bright, rosy red that I can't stop staring at. She looks like she just stepped off the cover of a 1950s magazine.

Her bright eyes stare back at me expectantly and I have to clear my throat to give myself a moment to think. "Okay. Miss Monroe –"

"Gabby," she cuts in. Her voice is smokey and it throws me off.

"Pardon?"

"My name is Gabby."

I stare at her a moment then nod. "Right. Gabby. I'm Sergeant Lawson. Constable Johnston is no longer going to be dealing with your case. I'm sorry that you had such a bad experience with him, but I will be taking over from here."

She nods, her hair bouncing around her shoulders as her head moves.

"So, Gabby. Tell me what's going on."

She leans forward in her seat, her face determined. "My brother hasn't been home in two days. He's nineteen." I say nothing, waiting for her to continue. She takes a deep breath and keeps going. "His name is Derrick. I know kids take off all the time, but Derrick wouldn't do that. He wouldn't leave without telling me where he was going." Tears fill her eyes. "We're all each other has," she whispers. Her eyes meet mine once more. "Something is wrong."

I nod. "Okay. So where was Derrick going the last time he left the house?"

She shrugs. "I don't know, really. He kind of comes and goes as he pleases. We both do."

"Was he with anyone?"

She shakes her head. "He was alone."

"Where does he normally go?"

Her face falls slightly and a tear slips from her eye and

slides down her cheek. "I don't know. I know he hangs out at a pool hall sometimes, but other than that, I have no clue. Oh, God." Her voice trembles. "I'm the worst big sister ever. I never ask where he goes. I do know he spends a lot of time with his friend Tommy. They've been inseparable since they were little kids."

I lean forward and catch her eyes. "Gabby, you're not the worst sister ever. Look, I'm not a big sister, but I am a big brother. If I asked my sister to report to me where she was going all the time, she'd kick my ass." I smirk and feel like a fucking champion when she smiles.

For the next forty-five minutes, I ask her every question I can think of to help me find her brother. I know that I need to turn this over to the Missing Persons Unit, but the more she talks, the more I think I can help her myself. I've been on the Street Crimes Unit now for a year and a half, and if there is one thing I know, it's the Crips. If Derrick is messed up with that street gang, I am the one that will find him. And I *will* find him.

When we're finished talking, I walk Gabby to the main entrance of the police station and stare down at her. She is much shorter than me — the top of her head barely meets my shoulder. "Okay, Gabby. I have your number on the paperwork you filled out." I hand her my card. "Now you have mine. If you hear anything that you think might be useful, please don't hesitate to call or text me, at any time. I will make sure to keep you up to date on this as well." She nods gratefully, her beautiful eyes once again filling with tears. I know I shouldn't touch her, but I can't help it. Reaching out, I take her hand and give it a squeeze, bending low until I meet her eyes. "We're gonna find him, Gabby."

She gives me a wobbly smile and nods before giving my hand a squeeze back. Then she lets go, turns and walks out of the building. I stand at the doorway and watch her go, trying not to focus on the sway of her ass or the motion of her dress against her hips as she walks. Once she's out of sight, I mentally give myself a shake and turn my thoughts to other matters. I head straight for the Chief's office. Time to deal with Frank.

Gabby

*W*alking into my empty house, my heart deflates when I realize that Derrick still isn't home. I hate how quiet it is here and I would give anything for him to just walk through that door. Our mother moved out of this house about a year ago, when her asshole boyfriend got a transfer to Alberta. She wanted us to go with her but we both refused. Now they're married, but that's okay because they live on the other side of the country and pretty much leave Derrick and me alone.

Since Mom left, I've been the one to kind of take care

of my brother. I pay the bills and buy the groceries, but luckily I don't have to worry about a mortgage because the house is paid for. That was the one smart thing Mom did. Derrick has it pretty easy. I don't ask much of him, other than to clean up after himself and take out the garbage. He even does it on occasion. I'm five years older than him and even though he's already graduated high school, the kid can't make a box of Kraft Dinner without burning the noodles to the bottom of the pot.

He does stuff for me too, though. He takes care of the yard in the summer and the snow in the winter, and I've never had to think about maintenance on my car because he takes care of that too. We're a team. And now he's gone and I don't know what to do.

Flopping down on the couch, I toss my purse aside and slip off my black slingback pumps, propping my tired feet up on the coffee table. I rest my head against the back of the couch and blow out a long breath. I don't know what else to do. I spent about an hour with Sergeant Lawson and, unlike his douchebag co-worker, I know he will do everything he can to find Derrick. But will it help?

Like I've done a million times in the last two days, I snatch up my purse, dig out my phone and dial my brother's cell. It rings five times before the voicemail picks up. "Hey, you've reached Derrick. I'm probably at home and screening my calls. Leave a message, and if you're lucky, I'll call ya back."

On the long beep, I squeeze my eyes closed and press the phone tighter to my ear. "Derrick? It's Gabby. Again. Just...Derrick, I'm scared. Please call me. I need to know that you're okay." I end the call and spend the next several seconds staring at my phone. And then I have an idea.

Jumping up, I dash up the stairs to Derrick's room and flip open his MacBook. I don't even bother checking his

Facebook or his email because he has both password protected, but I am able to access his contact list. Clicking on it, I scroll through the names until I find the one I'm looking for. Tommy Lewis.

Unlocking my iPhone once more, I tap out Tommy's phone number and hit send. It rings five times and then the voicemail picks up. "Talk to me!"

Sighing with frustration, I wait for the beep. "Tommy! This is Gabby. I really need to talk to you. I haven't heard from Derrick in two days now. I'm worried. Call me back, okay?" I leave him my phone number and hang up.

Taking a look around Derrick's room, my heart sinks even further. His room is disgusting, but that's nothing new. The thing that gets me most is the pictures taped to the wall. There are snapshots of his buddies and of him, and ones of him and girls and at parties. The pictures I love the most though are the ones of Derrick and me. There are several of them. Me and Derrick sitting on the dock at the lake when we were kids. The two of us, last year, sitting in the backyard with a beer in our hands. And my favourite, me and Derrick a few years ago when I was teaching him how to drive. The picture is taken from outside the car. He's sitting in the driver's seat with a huge grin on his face while I lean in from the passenger side, attempting to look terrified, but you can tell I'm laughing. Mom took that one.

God. Mom. I need to call her and tell her what's going on. Turning, I leave Derrick's room, close the door behind me and walk back down the stairs. I pull up my Mother's number and hit send. Yet again, after a few rings, I get her voicemail. At the beep, I leave my message.

"Mom, it's Gabby. Look, um…I just wanted you to know that, well…that Derrick hasn't been home in a couple of days and I'm starting to get really worried. Give me a call when you get this."

I end the call and flop back on the couch once again. I feel so lost and alone. My eyes fill with tears and I can't stop imagining all of the different and horrible things that could have happened to my brother.

Tears slide down my cheeks as I think about my mother and how she should be here to help me deal with this. I hate how selfish she is to have left us here on our own so she could go off and marry that asshole, Larry. But it's nothing new really. I know my Mom loves us in her own way, but she has always kind of been focused on her own life. We were an afterthought. Derrick and I have been taking care of ourselves in one way or another for years.

Sitting up, I take a deep, shaky breath and run my hands down my face to wipe away the tears. I need to smarten up. I need to stop whining and stop waiting for someone to help me. Derrick needs me. It's time to pull up my big girl panties and go find my brother.

Daniel

It's almost nine o'clock when I finally walk through my door. It was a long day at work. I'm tired and hungry and I need a goddamn beer. After Gabby left the station, I made the Chief aware of what had happened with Frank. It wasn't the first complaint he'd heard about Frank's lack of professionalism and he assured me that it would be handled. I just hope he's right.

Walking into my apartment, I head right for the fridge, crack open a beer and make myself a sandwich. I'm just smearing a thick layer of mayo on a slice of bread when my phone rings. I instantly recognize the ringtone as the one I've assigned for my sister, Laynie.

Dropping the knife on the counter, I move towards my

phone, licking mayo off my fingers. "Hello?"

"Hey Daniel! How are you?"

I smile at her easy tone, but my heart clenches just a little as I hear the proper words. My sister and I are close and I've always been protective of her. Years ago, Laynie and our brother Garrett had been on their way home from prom when their car was struck head on by a drunk driver. Laynie had suffered a head injury that had left her completely blind, and Garrett had died on impact. The crushing loss we'd suffered that fateful night had made our bond even stronger – but lately, things had been different. Laynie had met a guy and I don't like him one bit. This new boyfriend of hers is a biker, and a criminal, and the worst man possible for my baby sister.

Laynie does what she wants though. She's a strong woman and though she loves me, she does what she thinks is best for her, with or without my approval. I respect that, but it doesn't mean I have to like it.

"Hey Laynie. I'm good. What's up?"

"Nothing, really. Just called to say hi." She pauses and I wait, knowing there's more. "Oh, and Travis and I went to Mom and Dad's for the weekend. We just got back. Mom sent you something."

I raise my brows. She took *Travis* to our parent's house? I don't say anything, not wanting to piss her off. "What is it?"

"I don't know. I think it's a birthday present."

Rolling my eyes, I grab the plate with my sandwich, snag my beer then walk to the living room and sit on the couch. I arrange my supper on the coffee table and sit back with the phone still to my ear.

"Yeah. Probably. I've been busy lately and haven't been by to see them."

Laynie chuckles. "Yeah. She may have mentioned that

once or twice." I smirk, knowing that Mom probably whined about my absence the entire visit. "Anyways, since your birthday is in a couple of days she sent it home with us. She asked that we get it to you as soon as possible, so Travis is going to stop by with it in the morning. Will you be home?"

I cringe at the thought of that asshole even knowing where I live, let alone stopping by. "Yeah. I'll be here."

"Great!" Laynie sounds so happy — happier than I've ever heard her. Could it be that this asshole makes her happy? "And I was thinking! Since your birthday is in a couple of days, maybe you could come for supper?" She pauses for a moment and then sing songs, "I'll make your favourite."

I laugh. "Alright, I'll come. But I want chocolate cake. And I mean real chocolate cake this time. None of that gluten-free shit you made me last year."

Laynie's musical laughter echoes through the phone, making me smile. "Deal."

I finish up my conversation with my sister and then sit back to eat my supper. Flipping through channels, my mind wanders to Derrick Monroe. His sister seemed pretty worried about him, which makes me believe that she's right and something is definitely wrong. I passed the case off to the Missing Persons Unit, but that doesn't mean I can't do a little investigation of my own.

Looking around my bare apartment, I decide to do just that. There's a nightclub downtown where the Crips tend to hang out. There's no reason I can't go there myself, have a couple of drinks and maybe look around while I'm there. Maybe I'll even see Derrick.

Nodding at my own decision, I put my plate in the sink and head off to the shower. It doesn't take me long to get ready for a night on the town. A quick shower, shave and a splash of cologne and I'm off to the bar.

The line up outside is long for this time of night but it seems to be moving quickly. I only wait outside for about five minutes before the bouncer finally nods and lifts the rope, allowing me to enter the busy nightclub.

All around me, scantily dressed women squeal and laugh and dance and drink while the men stand around talking and looking tough while they down drinks of their own. Grabbing a drink from the bartender, I scan the crowd, instantly recognizing several gang members that are well-known to the police.

I'm just making my second scan across the room when I see her. Leaning up against a wall in the far corner, lips painted as red as her short, low-cut dress, is Gabby. And she's talking to a Crip.

Gabby

Maybe this wasn't such a good idea. I was sure that if I came here, where I know the Crips like to hang out, I would figure something out…or at least see Tommy. Now here I am, dressed in one of my sexiest red dresses, talking to a total creep.

I've never been one to be overtly flirty. I'm a take-me-as-I-am kind of girl. I'm a hairdresser with a unique style that tends to draw in the women, but freak out the men a little. I make friends easy enough, but I've never mastered the art of flirtation. Standing in this loud and crowded nightclub, I'm completely out of my element.

I'd been standing by the bar for an hour sipping on my Singapore Sling and trying to figure out who to talk to when a man approached me. I had never seen him before but he seemed friendly enough, and I can tell by the blue he's wearing and the tattoos on his arms that he's a Crip.

Three drinks and a whole lot of lame pickup lines later, I'm no closer to learning anything at all about my brother, and I am now in a situation where I can't walk away from this guy without making a scene. I look up at him and bat my eyelashes, hoping I look flirtatious and not like I have something stuck in there. He grins down at me, assuming I liked whatever the hell he just said.

Uh oh. What had he just said to me? Just then, he leans in close and wraps his arm around my hips, dragging my body into his. *Fuck.* His nose fits itself into the crook of my neck and I barely contain my yelp when his tongue flicks out, tasting my bare skin. *Shit. Think Gabby! Think!*

"What the fuck! Baby, I've been looking everywhere for you! What are you doing?"

I look up in surprise and am thrown backwards a little when tongue boy whips around to face whoever had spoken. *Double shit.* It's Sergeant Lawson…and he doesn't look happy. The guy I was with takes a step forward and pokes him hard in the chest.

"Who the fuck are you?"

Sergeant Lawson plants his feet and raises his eyebrow at him. He towers over the younger man and easily outweighs him by forty pounds of solid muscle. "I'm her man. Who the fuck are you?"

Tongue boy screws his face up and turns to give me a dirty look. "Fuck this shit, man. Stupid bitch." He gives me one last sneer and then pushes past Sergeant Lawson and disappears into the crowd of dancing bodies.

I probably look like a complete fool with my eyes wide and my mouth hanging open, but I can't help it. *What the hell is he doing here anyway? And why does he smell so good?* It hadn't escaped my notice earlier today that he is one of the most gorgeous men I've ever seen in real life, but at the time I was pissed off and was focused on getting the missing persons report filed.

Now that I've had a few drinks and feel a little looser, I can't help but notice how perfect those jeans mould to his muscular thighs, or how hot he looks in that green button-down shirt.

Sergeant Lawson's eyes narrow on me. "Gabby? What the hell are you doing here?"

I stare at him a beat, my mouth still hanging open. "I, uh …" Swallowing, I decide to stop looking at his body and start looking at just his eyes. *Fuck. Look at how green they are.* "Um…I just …" I got nothing. In an attempt to salvage this situation and avoid looking like a stuttering fool, I shrug and just grin at him.

His jaw hardens and his eyes narrow further. "Are you out of your mind? You're here looking for information on your brother, aren't you?" I swallow again and nod. He shakes his head and glares at me. "You *are* out of your mind. Do you have any idea how badly this could have gone, Gabby? These guys aren't good people. They're not just gonna tell you where he is! They could have figured you out! You could have been hurt!"

His anger confuses me. "I wasn't doing anything dangerous. I was just trying to find out some information."

"Not dangerous? Are you fucking kidding me right now?" He grabs my arm and pulls me close, his mouth close to my ear. "This bar is fucking crawling with gang members, Gabby. The same gang members that may or may not have done something to your brother. Use your head!"

My eyes widen and I yank myself out of his grasp. "Excuse me! I appreciate your concern, Sergeant Lawson, but —"

"Daniel," he barks.

I stare at him, surprised by the interruption. "Fine. Whatever. I appreciate your concern, *Daniel*, but I'm a grown woman. I can take care of myself, thank you very much. Now if you'll excuse me, I have some people to talk to."

He grabs my arm again. "I don't think so, Gabby. You need to take a step back and let the police do their job. We are trained to deal with this shit. You're not."

As he talks, my anger grows, but I find it harder and harder to focus on his words. The room spins slowly and my skin starts to feel hot and clammy. When I look at him to give him my best glare, there is two of him.

"I can't wait around for you la —" My words are cut off as my knees give out. Just as I'm about to hit the floor, Daniel wraps his arm around me, dragging me up to my feet once more. My head rolls loosely on my neck and I struggle to keep my eyes open. Something is very wrong.

"Gabby? Gabby!" I can hear him calling me, but the sound is muffled — echoing somehow, like it's coming from far away. My eyes fall closed and no matter how hard I try, I can't peel them apart again. The last thing I hear is Daniel calling my name.

Daniel

Last night did not go as planned. When Gabby collapsed, I caught her just before she hit the floor. She showed definite signs of being drugged. The date rape drug acts fast and, luckily for her, I came along before that greasy thug got his chance to touch her.

I made quick work of getting her out of that club and into my car. I didn't know what to do with her. I knew that someone needed to keep an eye on her, so I just brought her to my house. She spent over an hour throwing up before I finally managed to get her into my bed.

Now it's morning and I'm in the kitchen making breakfast, waiting for her to wake up. This is not good. She's sleeping in my bed. This is not good. There's no way I should have allowed things to get this personal with her, but what else could I do?

Thinking back to last night, I remember how fast my blood heated when I saw that fucker put his hands on her. It was all I could do to stay calm and not rip him to shreds. I'm pissed at her too. I know she wants to find her brother, but she's obviously clueless of just how dangerous the Crips are. You don't fuck with them without them fucking you right back.

A noise in the hallway breaks me from my thoughts and I look up just as Gabby peers cautiously around the corner. When she sees me, her eyes widen and I can hear her gasp from across the room.

"Sergeant Lawson?" She steps into the room and looks around, her dress wrinkled and hair tousled. Her eye makeup is smudged around her eyes giving her a slightly raccoon-type appearance. It doesn't even matter. She still looks beautiful.

"Daniel. Call me Daniel." She stares at me, nibbling on her lower lip. Breaking the silence, I raise my coffee cup. "Coffee?"

She curls her lip. "No thank you. I don't drink coffee." Her eyes scan the open concept living room/dining room/kitchen combo before coming back to me. "Um.

Daniel? Why am I here?"

Sighing heavily, I stand from my spot and take a few steps towards her. "Well, I went to the club last night, hoping to get some information on your brother's whereabouts when guess who I should see there. Any guesses?" Her eyes narrow but she says nothing. "That's right, Gabby. I see you. Snuggled up with a Crip. And not just any Crip, but a Crip who was carrying a handy stash of roofies." Her eyes widen in surprise and my anger grows as I talk, just thinking of how close she came to being hurt. "You're lucky I came along when I did or you'd be waking up somewhere a lot worse than my place...if you woke up at all."

"I was roofied?" I stare at her and nod, glad she's finally getting that her move last night was crazy and dangerous. "Wow," she says as she walks the rest of the way into the kitchen. "Thank you for helping me, Daniel." I nod again, considering the conversation over. "I do appreciate it, but I'll tell you right now, I don't appreciate the way you're talking to me." I stare at her in surprise. "I was only there because sitting around doing nothing isn't getting me anywhere. I can't sit in that empty house another minute when I could be doing something to find my brother."

I take another couple of steps towards her, until I am close enough to touch her. "I get that Gabby, but you need to think things through! You made a stupid move last night."

Her eyes narrow, and her voice lowers. "Don't you ever call me stupid."

Sighing, I reach for her. "I didn't mean it like that." She jerks out of my reach and I groan, stabbing my fingers through my hair. "Look, I'm a cop. I know what I'm doing here. You shouldn't have been there. Next time you try something like that, I won't hesitate to redden your ass." I don't know who's more shocked that I said it, but I meant it.

She frowns and glares at me. "You're as big of an asshole as that Frank guy from the station!"

Her anger doesn't phase me. The truth is, after saying what I said, I can't get the image of her bent over in front of me, my reddened handprint shining bright on her pale skin. Before I get a chance to respond, a knock on the door breaks the tension. We both turn to stare at it, our argument temporarily forgotten. *Who the hell could it be? It's barely eight thirty in the morning.*

Turning, I stride toward the door and look through the peep hole. *Fuck.* It's my sister's thug boyfriend. I forgot he was coming over. Pulling open the door, I ignore Gabby behind me, and hope to make this quick.

"Travis," I greet.

He nods silently and holds out a wrapped package. I look up to see another man on a bike, idling at the side of the road. Bikers. Travis is a member of the Kings of Korruption MC and goes by the name Tease. I instantly recognize the man at the corner as Bosco, the King's newest prospect. I've been profiling the Kings for over a year now, so it's no surprise that I hate my sister being tangled up with this guy.

"Tell Laynie I said thank you," I say.

He nods again. "Will do." Turning, he takes a single step down the stairs to head back to his bike when Gabby rushes out the door, knocking me out of her way. She charges past Travis and heads straight for Bosco.

I watch in shock as she says something to him, her arms gesturing wildly. He stares at her in surprise, his eyes amused, before he shrugs and nods. Gabby throws her leg over the back of his bike and climbs on. I break out of my daze and hurry down the steps to the sidewalk. Just when I reach it, Bosco revs his motor and peels off down the street. I watch in anger and desperation as he carries her away, and am shocked even further when Gabby turns around and raises her arm, staring right at me as she gives me the finger.

A chuckle from behind me reminds me that Travis is still standing there. "Damn, man. You pissed that bitch off."

"Where's he taking her?" I demand, turning and getting in his space.

He smirks. "I don't have a fuckin' clue, man but you best take a step back. Whatever you did to piss her off is not my problem." He steps around me and walks towards his bike. "Look. If you want, I'll go to the clubhouse and see what I can find out, okay?"

I grit my teeth and nod, not wanting to rely on his help with anything, but not having much choice in the matter. Travis nods in return and climbs onto his ride, leaving without another word.

I stare after him, my mind racing. The Kings are notorious around here for being more dangerous than the Crips. Hell, they're the most dangerous club in the country. Surely Gabby wasn't that clueless to think that she'd be safe with them. But she must be, because why else would she ride off on the back of a bike belonging to a King?

Gabby

Okay, maybe leaving with this biker wasn't the best idea, but when I'd seen the Kings of Korruption logo on his leather cut, the idea came to me and I ran with it. Besides, Daniel was being an asshole. Admittedly, he was probably right, and I probably just proved him right again that I have a tendency to not think things through. It doesn't matter though. I have been impulsive all my life. I know how to handle myself.

The bike pulls to a stop in front of a large building surrounded by motorcycles. The front part of the building seems to be a garage and there are several tattooed, hairy men milling about talking and working on cars and bikes. I look around in awe, taking it all in.

"You gonna get off the bike, Sweet pea?"

His voice startles me, and I swing my eyes to his. He sits in front of me on the bike, his torso turned so he can look at me, a smirk plastered on his handsome face. My eyes widen and I scramble off the bike, instantly aware of how dishevelled I look. My hair is still a mess, my makeup is likely smeared across my face from the night before and my dress is rumpled. He laughs at my awkward dismount and gracefully gets off himself.

"Come on, girl," he says on a chuckle. He grabs my hand in his and starts walking towards a door near the back of the building. Bikers are everywhere and it seems every eye is on me as we walk.

"Um…" *Shit. I don't know this guy's name.* "Sir?"

He turns and stares at me, bursting into laughter. "Sir? Alright, I can deal with that. What can I do for you, Ma'am?"

My cheeks flame. "Maybe this isn't such a good idea." I tug on my hand, attempting to pull it from his. "I think I'll just go home, actually. Thanks for the ride, but …" My voice trails off as I stare at where my hand is trapped in his.

"Look, Sweet pea. If you are who you say you are, this is definitely a good idea." He sighs and squeezes my hand. "Listen, just go in there and say what you gotta say, and if after that if you still want to leave I'll take you home myself, okay?"

I stare at him, my eyes filling with tears, and nod. My heart pounds in my chest. I don't know if I can do this. I don't know if I *should* do this. Reluctantly, I follow him. I don't have much choice seeing as my hand is still trapped in his. He gently guides me through the door and into the building. We enter directly into a room that looks just like a seedy bar. Considering it's barely nine o'clock in the morning, there is nobody around.

He walks me even farther, pulling me down a long and narrow hall. I look around, trying to ignore my pounding heart as I take in everything around me. Finally, he comes to a stop just outside a wooden door at the end of the hall. Knocking on it, my breath catches in my chest while we wait for an answer.

"Come in."

The voice comes from inside and my heart jumps into my throat, racing the entire time. I tug on my hand again as the biker pushes the door open, but he just gives it a reassuring squeeze and pulls me inside.

The room is large and dingy, paperwork stacked untidily on every surface. The walls are covered in naked and half-naked women, and a large wooden desk sits off toward the back of the room. It's the man behind that desk that is causing my body to tremble.

He looks almost exactly the same as he did the last time I'd seen him — back when I was only six years old. Sure, he's a little older looking and has more tattoos than he did back then, but there's no doubt that this is him.

The man stands slowly, his brow furrowed in frustration. "What the fuck, Bosco? You know I don't let bitches back here! Who the hell is this?"

My body locks tight at the sound of his voice. If there was ever any doubt in my mind, it's completely gone now. I still hear that voice in my sleep sometimes.

"Funny you should ask," Bosco drawls. He turns to me and gives me a reassuring smile. "I'll be out in the hall."

Staring into his eyes, I nod gratefully, glad that he's not abandoning me entirely. Bosco nods in return and winks before he backs out of the room and closes the door. I stare at that door, wishing I could run through it myself and never look back. But I'm here now, and this is my best shot. I need to take it.

Turning, I face the angry looking man behind the desk and paste on a phony smile. "Hi Daddy," I whisper.

Daniel

As much as I hate my sister's boyfriend, he'd been decent enough to text me this morning to let me know that Gabby was safe. About an hour ago I received another text from him, letting me know that she would be home shortly.

So here I sit, on her front step, waiting. I can't believe she just hopped on the back of that guy's bike and took off. And gave me the finger. We will definitely be talking about that. I don't know what it is about this girl that gets me so uptight but when she left with him, I just about went crazy. If it weren't for Travis reassuring me that she was fine, I just may have.

The roar of a motorcycle snaps me from my thoughts. I look up from my spot and see Gunner, the president of the Kings of Korruption MC, pull up with Gabby on the back of his motorcycle. Her eyes widen when she sees me, but she says nothing. I stand from where I'm sitting and watch as she climbs off the bike and the two exchange a few words that I can't hear from where I am. I watch as Gunner says something to her, his face soft. She nods her head and turns to face me. Over her shoulder, Gunner narrows his eyes at me and shakes his head. Then he pulls away from the curb and is gone.

I look to Gabby and see her approaching. "What are you doing here, Daniel?"

I walk towards her, slowing to a stop when I get to where she stands with her hands on her hips. I know she's still pissed at me for this morning, but I don't care. I'm pissed at her, too. Her narrowed eyes and angry posture just about pushes me over the edge. Grabbing her arms, I pull her into me and look down into her angry eyes. "Fuck, Gabby! I was fucking worried! What the hell? Do you ever think before you do crazy shit?"

She stands on her tiptoes, getting right back into my space, eyes flaming. "Yes I think! And why do you even care? Your job is to find my brother, not play babysitter to me!"

I don't know what makes me angrier. The fact that I still don't know why the hell she went to the Kings or the fact that she's right. What she does *is* none of my business — *so why do I care?* "Why were you with the Kings?" I snarl.

"Because Gunner is my father," she snarls right back.

We both freeze. *Her father? Gunner Monroe is Gabby's father?* She's still up on her tiptoes, looking slightly less angry, but still not backing down. I realize now that her chest is pressed against mine and we're both breathing heavily, causing our chests to brush against each other.

"Your father? Why didn't you tell me that?" I ask, all my anger is gone and now I'm just confused. I profiled Gunner Monroe myself and never once had I discovered that he had children.

She drops back to her feet, moving herself out of my space and nods. "Because I haven't seen or spoken to him since I was six years old. I didn't even think of it until I saw that biker on your front step. When I saw that younger one sitting on his bike, I just told him who I was and that I needed him to take me to my father." Her eyes fill with tears. "Asking Gunner for help was one of the hardest things I've ever done."

Her impulsive actions in the last twenty-four hours, while admittedly crazy, kind of make sense. The girl is desperate to find her brother. If Laynie ever went missing, I'd stop at nothing to find her.

Taking her hand, I lead her to the front step of her house and together we sit side by side. "What did he say?" I ask, careful to keep my voice gentle.

She sniffs and wipes away a stray tear. "He was happy to see me. When I told him about Derrick, he said he'd help right away. I think he's worried too, which is weird considering he hasn't even seen Derrick since he was about a year old." A sad smile flits across her face. "When I was six and my brother was just a baby, my parents fought…a lot." The quiver in her voice makes me want to pull her into my arms and comfort her, but I don't. I sense she needs to tell me this on her own. "Since I've grown up, I've learned that my mom wasn't happy with my father's biker lifestyle. She gave him an ultimatum, and he chose the Kings. After he left he sent money to my mother every month, but at her request, he never attempted to contact us."

I reach out and wipe away another tear from her cheek. Having been raised in a stable home with both parents, I can only imagine what she is going through, how much courage it took to go to him after he'd abandoned them like that. "Gabby, you didn't need to do that. You don't need them. I'm *going* to find Derrick for you."

She snorts without humour. "You can't promise me that." Her eyes meet mine. "Look, Daniel, I know I shouldn't have gone to them, and I know that they're way of doing things is a little …" She looks off to the right as she searches for the right word. "Different than yours, but I need to know that I'm doing everything I can to find him. I'm the only one that even notices he's missing. I'm all he has, and he's all I have."

I barely even know this woman, but seeing her so worried tears me apart. I hate that sad look on her face. I hate knowing the desperation she feels. Reaching over, I wrap my arm around her and pull her into my side. "I can't promise you that I'll find him, but I can promise you that I'll do everything I can. And if that fails, I'll do even more."

She looks over at me then, a ghost of a smile playing across her full lips. "Thank you, Daniel. And I'm sorry I gave you the finger."

I chuckle. "Yeah, that wasn't very nice." She laughs with me and nudges me with her shoulder.

"You were right, though," she says. "I'm kind of impulsive." She gives me a sheepish grin. "I tend to act first, think later."

I feign shock. "You don't say!"

We both chuckle, but the chuckle quickly fades for both of us and we end up staring into each other's eyes. I know I shouldn't be here. I know I shouldn't touch her. But it's like I have no control. I'm drawn to her.

Reaching out, I tip her chin up and move in closer. "Trust me, okay?" She nods, and I hear her swallow thickly. Her eyes are glued to my lips. Moving in, I brush my lips lightly against hers. "And no more crazy shit. Got it?"

She nods again, and I just smile, our lips barely touching. I'm about to pull away, not wanting to take advantage of her worry when she leans forward and presses her lips against mine. I freeze for a second, not sure what to do. When her hands come up and grasp my hair, I decide to go for it. Leaning into the kiss, I part my lips against hers.

When she pulls me even closer, I realize how bad this looks. An officer taking advantage of a civilian outside in the open. Pulling back, I paste on a smile. "Now that I know you're okay, I have some work to do. Go inside and relax. I'll let you know what I find out."

She stares at me and nods, and I can't help myself. I lean in and give her another soft brush with my lips. Pulling back, I smile. I wait for her to get inside her house and then try to ignore my erection as I walk to my car.

Gabby

*I*t's hard to believe it's only three o'clock in the afternoon. So much has happened today. I woke up in a strange bed, jumped onto the back of a strange biker's motorcycle, flipped off a sexy cop, confronted my estranged father, and then kissed that same sexy cop. The kiss was the best part.

I just met Daniel yesterday, but already we have been through a lot together. Sure, he's bossy, which pisses me off, but I feel safe with him. It's strange really, because I don't feel safe with any man. No man, including my father, has ever given me reason to. Neither has my mother for that matter. I have always been my own safety net. So how come just two days with Daniel makes me want to finally trust someone else to do the job for me?

I walk into the bathroom, my thoughts swirling, but I stop in my tracks when I see my reflection. *Good God! Is this what I've looked like all day?* I look scary. *And I kissed Daniel like this!*

Flipping on the shower, I start peeling off my rumpled clothes and jump inside. The water beats against my skin, doing little to wash away the tension I feel. After getting out, I go about my regular beauty routine, put my mass of curls up with a red bandana and pair my look with a cute little sundress I bought at a second-hand store last week.

I open the fridge to make myself something to eat, but am quickly reminded by the bare shelves that I haven't had time to get to the grocery store this week. The cupboards are just as bare. Deciding the fresh air would do me some good, I slip on my shoes, grab my purse and walk the three blocks to the nearest café.

The Bean has a Caramel Macchiato that is sure to wake me up. I order the largest size and pair it with a Tuscan turkey wrap. The cashier writes my name on the tall plastic cup and I move to the line-up of people waiting for their orders to be made.

The bell on the door dings just as a trio young men spill inside, laughter echoing around the small coffee shop. Everyone eyes them uncomfortably, taking in their blue clothing and rough exterior. Crips. I look at the three men, foolishly hoping that one is Derrick. My heart flips when my eyes land on the third man.

Rushing forward, I grab his arm and pull him off to the side. "Tommy! I've been trying to reach you!" I keep talking, not even noticing when he yanks his arm from my grasp. "Derrick hasn't been home in –"

"Bitch, you need to back the fuck off me," he says, his face distorted in annoyance. "I didn't call you back because I didn't want to fuckin' talk to you." He glances back at the two guys he came in with, shaking his head in disgust. The two men eye us both, tension crowding the room in an instant.

I stare at him is shock. "*What* did you just say to me?"

"Bitch, you heard me. I know why you fuckin' called. I just don't care. Now if you don't mind, I'm here to get a coffee and then me and the boys got shit to do."

I grasp the front of his shirt and yank his body to mine. "You listen here you little shit. It wasn't so long ago that I used to wipe the SpagettiO's off your chin because your mother was too drunk to feed you. You remember that, Tommy?" I motion to the guys behind him and lower my voice. "You want to be tough in front of your boys, that's your deal. But I swear to God, if you don't tell me what happened to my brother, I will rip your balls off with my bare hands and use them to flavour your coffee. You hear me?"

He stares down at me as I speak, the anger in his face replaced with sadness for just a flash and then it's gone. After a moment, he yanks himself out of my grasp and shakes his head. "Yeah I hear ya, Gabby. But if you were smart, you'd just let it go. Your brother got what was coming to him. It's done now. Don't get yourself involved. Do *you* hear *me?*"

I stare back at him, my eyes wide. What does that mean? Before I even get a chance to ask, Tommy shakes his head and walks out of the coffee shop, his buddies right on his heels and the barista is calling my name.

I don't even approach the counter. My head spinning, I

head for home, Tommy's words playing over and over in my head. *Your brother got what was coming to him. It's done now.* What the fuck did he mean? Tears cloud my vision as I close the door to my house. Pressing my back against it, I sink to the floor, wracked with harsh, gasping sobs.

Daniel

My phone rings from an unknown number just as I'm finishing up my paperwork. "Hello?"

"Lawson?"

I don't recognize the gruff voice. "Yeah."

"Gunner Monroe." My body freezes. What the fuck would Gunner have to say to me?

"What can I help you with Mr. Monroe?"

"Well, Officer Lawson –"

"Sergeant. It's Sergeant Lawson."

He chuckles. "Okay. Sergeant Lawson…I couldn't help but notice that you were sitting on my daughter's doorstep when I dropped her off earlier. Are house calls a service that all city cops offer?"

I grit my teeth. "What's your point Monroe?"

"Bosco also informed me that she came running out of *your* place this very morning. Is that true?"

I sigh. "That's none of your business."

An angry silence fills the line. "That's my daughter, Lawson. I'd say that makes it my business."

"Well, sir, I disagree. I met Gabby yesterday and I bet you that I already know her a hell of a lot better than you do. Now if you don't mind getting to the point, I have work to do."

"Fuck you, Lawson. You're lucky your sister is family,

or I'd have fucked you over months ago. Stay out of our shit and we won't have any problems. That also means stay the fuck away from my daughter." My jaw hardens at his tone. "Gabby and Derrick are family, and the Kings will find my son. We take care of our own."

I snort. "Yeah. Sounds like you've done a great job when it comes to your kids. Look...the Kings are already being watched. I tell you that as a brother, scared for his sister, not a cop to a criminal. Let the cops do their jobs Monroe, and keep your boys out of trouble."

I disconnect the call without waiting for a response. I'm just stuffing it back into my pocket when it rings again.

"Hello?" I drawl, sure that it's Gunner calling to get the last word.

"Daniel?" Her voice is filled with tears and barely understandable. My gut clenches.

"Gabby! What's wrong? Are you okay?"

She sobs softly. "I went..." She sobs again, her voice muffled. "I ..." She blows her nose and I hear her take a deep breath. "Sorry...I went to the coffee shop to grab a late lunch. When I was there, Tommy walked in." Her voice wavers again. "I tried to talk to him and he told me to back off. He said that—" I can hear the exact second she loses what little control she had, but she pushes through, her voice heavy with tears. "He said that Derrick got what was coming to him and that it's done now." Another sob takes over. "What the hell does that even mean Daniel?"

It means that Derrick is in serious trouble, that's what it means, but I'm not about to tell Gabby that. "I don't know, baby. Where are you right now?"

She sniffs. "Home. I called you as soon as I got back."

I stand up, already moving to my car. "Okay, baby. You hold tight. I'll be there in ten minutes."

"No, Daniel. You don't have to do that."

"I said, I'll be there in ten minutes. No arguments."

Another sniff. "Okay. But Daniel?" I swing into my car and start it up, waiting for her to argue again. "Can you bring me something to eat. I'm hungry and I never did get my Tuscan turkey wrap or my macchiato."

I chuckle as I pull out of my parking spot. "Yeah, babe. I'll bring you some food."

I hear a small smile in her still sad voice as she whispers, "See you soon."

I disconnect the call and drive down the street, pushing the Bluetooth button and directing it to call dispatch.

"Ottawa City Police. How may I help you?"

"Hey, Nancy. Lawson, here. I need you to look up a Tommy Lewis for me. Approximately 19 years old. Lives on the west side. I need everything you can find on this kid. Address, known hangouts, priors, any warrants — everything. I'll call back in a bit and get the info from ya."

"You got it Sergeant Lawson. I'll see what I can find."

"Thanks Nancy." I disconnect and tap my fingers on the steering wheel. This Tommy kid and I need to have a little chat.

Gabby

*W*aiting for Daniel to show up at my house gives me a little time to settle down. Now I'm just angry. Tommy and
Derrick have been best friends since the day they started
school, fifteen years ago. Over the years he spent way more
time in our house than he did in his own. I hadn't been lying when I reminded him about how I fed him. I have. For
years I have.

Tommy's mother is an alcoholic who has never had
much use for her son. At least at our house, I was able to
make sure he was fed, and when he was younger, I even
bathed him. Our own mother may not have had a lot of

time for us, but in her own flighty way I always knew she loved us. Tommy couldn't say the same. I cared for Tommy like a little brother and had quickly accepted responsibility for him when I was basically just a kid myself.

That's what made his words even worse today. It was like a slap to the face after all those years I spent caring for him when he needed someone to do just that. Sitting here, stewing in my anger, I think over all the things I should've said or done differently. I should have slapped his mouth and kicked his ass. I should have chased him down and told him off. Funny how these ideas always seem to come to you long after the situation that pissed you off in the first place is over.

The doorbell chimes and I jump up from my spot on the couch, running down the narrow hallway to answer it. When I open the door, Daniel enters with a delicious looking iced cappuccino and a bag from Tim Horton's. Holding it up, he grins, his eyes crinkling a little in the corners. "Your dinner, m'lady."

For the first time, I notice just how blue his eyes really are. It catches me off guard. I'm unable to look away. "Thanks," I say, suddenly feeling a little breathless. His head tilts to the side a little and suddenly my breathing becomes harder to control as I take in the heat in his eyes. I feel like I'm under his spell.

He breaks that spell with a soft chuckle and a smirk before turning me away from him and guiding me to my couch with his hand pressed against the small of my back. "Eat."

I ignore my red cheeks and do as I'm told. I sit on the couch and pull two delicious looking sandwiches from the bag. Daniel reaches over and takes one, neatly unwrapping the paper from the sandwich. Side by side we sit on the couch, enjoying our food in a comfortable silence. I don't know about him, but after all that happened last night and today, the only thing I'm concerned about right now is how quickly I can get this sandwich into my belly.

I finish my meal and am just draining the last of my cappuccino when Daniel wads up his napkin and tosses it on the table. Leaning back on the couch, I watch as his large hand comes up and pats his stomach. I watch every move that hand makes, the fact that his stomach looks like a washboard under that shirt is not escaping me either.

"So, tell me what happened."

"Huh?" My shoulders jerk in surprise and my eyes slide from their place on his abs, up his well-defined chest, past his chiselled jawline and full lips, and lock onto his. He smirks a little then, totally not missing the fact that I was just staring at his muscles.

"At the coffee shop. What happened?"

Instantly, I'm pissed all over again. I run through the scene with him, telling him everything that was said. "What did he even mean? He got what was coming to him?"

"I don't know, Gabby. But it doesn't sound good." My heart squeezes. Deep down, I know that's the case, but hearing Daniel say it scares me even more. "So, you said Tommy seemed angry. Angry at you?"

I think back, trying to remember every detail. "Yeah. For the most part he seemed annoyed that I was even talking to him. He sounded pissed off and his body language was like he was ready to snap ..." The memory of Tommy's face when I reminded him of who I was to him flashes through my mind. "But for just a second there, he seemed almost sad." I look at Daniel, my eyes searching his, as though I would find my answers there. "Like he didn't want to be fighting with me like that. Do you think it's possible that he was just putting on a show?"

Daniel reaches out, his thumb skimming along my

cheekbone. "I don't know Gabby. But I'm going to find out. As soon as I leave here, I'm gonna hunt down this Tommy kid myself and get some answers."

Instantly I feel foolish. Avoiding his eyes, I look down at my lap and pick at a few pieces of imaginary lint. "Daniel, I'm so sorry for making you feel like you had to come here and check on me. I know you have a job to do, and I was acting like a total basket case. I feel silly."

"You don't get it, do you?" I stop my picking and look up at him, my brow furrowed in confusion. "Do you think all cops do this stuff for the family of a missing person?"

I don't take my eyes off his as I bite my lip and shake my head. I know they don't.

"Gabby, I'm here because you needed me here, whether you want to admit it or not. I like you, and when the opportunity presents itself to save the damsel in distress with a fast food sandwich and a coffee, I'm gonna take it. I get the feeling you don't let that happen very often."

God. My eyes move from his intense stare to his lips, my face heats up as he moves his face even closer to mine. I look up and meet his eyes, my heart racing in my chest. Deciding to just go for it before I lose my nerve, I reach up and grab the sides of his face and press my lips against his.

For just a fraction of a second he doesn't move, and my heart sinks. Beating back the fear of rejection I'm already battling, I lean into him even more and slide my lips across his, praying that he'll kiss me back — and then he does. Daniel's hands come up and press against the sides of my face, holding me right where I am. His tongue slides out and glides along the seam of my lips. My entire body shivers as I slide my own tongue along his, tasting him.

Deepening the kiss, I move even closer until my chest is pressed tight against his. My heart pounds an unsteady rhythm and my head swims as I struggle to catch my breath. Daniel's lips dance with mine, returning my kiss with as much passion as I feel. His hot breath collides with my own in soft pants and gasps.

I feel his fingers working in my hair and suddenly my bandana is gone and my hair tumbles down around my shoulders. Daniel's fingers tangle themselves deep into it, guiding me down as he leans his long body back on the couch. Swinging a leg over him, I never break my lips from his as I straddle him.

Wearing only a dress and a pair of silky panties, I find that in this position I can feel every hard and wanting inch of him pressed exactly where I want it. Rotating my hips, I nip and suck and bite at his lips, swallowing down his deep groan. His hands slide down my body and grasp my hips, guiding me into a gentle rocking rhythm. My panties are soaked as his length glides back and forth over my clit.

Daniel lifts his head from the arm of the couch and takes over the kiss. I kiss him back, desperately moaning and gasping above him as he sucks and nips at me, rocking me back and forth against him, knowing exactly what he is doing to me. Heat builds in my clit as my orgasm draws closer.

Daniel groans again and pulls his lips from mine, pushing me back so I'm sitting up on his lap. His eyes burn into mine as he pulls his hand from my hip and slides my dress up, exposing my panties. "I want to fuck you so bad right now, Gabby."

I respond by rolling my hips, hitting my clit once more on the enormous bulge in his pants. My teeth sink deep into my lip and his eyes flare. Placing both hands on my inner thighs, he spreads my legs wide. "You wanna cum baby, you cum my way." His words come out more like a growl.

I can't contain my gasp when he yanks aside my panties, the cool air hitting my hot and needy pussy. "Fuck, baby," he grinds out, his voice thick and husky. "Look at you."

He reaches out with one finger and slowly slides it through my wetness. I roll my hips, gasping when his finger grazes my clit. Then, finally, his finger is pushing deep inside of me, his thumb pressing against the swollen bundle of nerves. "Ride my finger, Gabby."

Staring down at him, I do as I'm told, riding his finger, my pussy gripping it tight. I watch as his eyes slide back and forth between my eyes and where his hand is working me. His cheeks are flushed and his chest rises and falls rapidly. The heat in my clit builds hotter and hotter until my body starts to tremble. His thumb works harder and his eyes lock on mine. And then I'm falling.

Pressing my hands to his chest, I let my head fall back and I cum harder than I've ever cum before, slowing my hips as my body shakes and jerks on top of him. As the wave passes and my body slows, I tip my head down and see Daniel staring up at me.

"You're beautiful, Gabby," he says.

I feel the heat hit my cheeks. "Thank you," I whisper, suddenly very shy.

He pulls his hand away and smiles up at me. "Kiss me." I blink at him, still in a bit of a daze. He chuckles softly and swings his legs off the couch, taking my body with him as he sits up, our faces now inches apart. "Never mind."

His mouth claims mine in a hard and fast kiss, clouding what little sense I have left. Just when I'm about to lean into him again, his lips are gone and he quickly replaces it with his thumb, pressing it against my swollen lips. His eyes bore into mine and a small smile ghosts across his face.

"I hate to do this Gabby, but I gotta go." I try to open my mouth to protest, but he keeps his thumb in place and shakes his head. "No, I do. If I had my way, I'd lay you down and take you right now, baby. But I'm a good guy. And the fact is, your brother is still missing." My confusion fades and it feels as if he's just thrown a bucket of cold water on me. "Taking advantage of you when you're vulnerable isn't my style. And I need to get the fuck out of here before I forget that." He lands one last swift kiss on my lips, then moves me to the side and stands. I watch with wide eyes as he adjusts himself inside his pants and turns back to me.

I say nothing, just staring up at him. All over again, I feel like the worst sister ever. My brother is missing and here I am, riding the cop that's supposed to be out there looking for him. *What am I doing?* "I'm gonna find him, baby. And when he's back, and you're happy, we are going to finish what we just started."

Daniel

It takes the entire drive to Tommy Lewis's house for my dick to calm the fuck down. Watching Gabby ride my fingers is a sight I will never forget for as long as I live. *Fuck.* She is so different from any girl I've ever been attracted to. Even though it's only been a couple of days since I met her, I just can't picture myself ever wanting anyone else.

I've always been into girls that are beautiful in a more subtle, quiet way. Girls that rarely argue and tend to have their noses stuck in books. Gabby is different. She's beautiful and vibrant, her hair and makeup done up a way that makes her stand out. She's far from quiet and is easily the most impulsive person I've ever met. It's refreshing.

I double check the detailed text, complete with mug shots, that Nancy in dispatch sent me. Walking up the steps to the Lewis residence, I note the unkempt grass and the garbage piled high on the front step. The sound of a TV blaring inside filters through the door. I ring the doorbell and wait. Still I hear just the sound of the TV. I ring it again. Still nothing. On the third ring, I finally hear some-one curse from inside followed by footsteps.

The door swings open, and I'm greeted by a paper thin woman with wild, greasy brown hair, and a lit cigarette in her hand. Her face is wrinkled and her mouth in sunken in from her lack of teeth. "Yeah?" she says, her voice showing her years of heavy smoking.

I show her my badge and watch as her eyes widen. "I'm Sergeant Lawson, ma'am. I'm looking for a Tommy Lewis. I know he lives here. Is he home?"

Her eyes slide from my badge, back to me. I can tell by her glazed look that she's wasted, but she answers me clearly. "Yeah, he lives here, but the little fucker's out. Took my last pack of smokes too. Bastard."

"You don't happen to know where I might find him, do you?"

She purses her lips and her eyes drift off to the side as she thinks. "He's probably out with that Derrick kid some-where. Maybe at the pool hall. Those boys spend a lot of time down there."

"You don't happen to know the name of that pool hall, do you?" I watch as her body sways, standing getting to be too difficult in her drunken state.

"No idea. But it's the one on the corner of Williams Street."

I nod, knowing exactly where she's talking about. "I know just where it is. Thank you Ms. Lew —" I don't even get to finish my thanks before the door slams shut in my face. Shaking my head, I turn and hurry down the steps to my car. *Poor Tommy. Any kid would be fucked up with a*

Mom like that.

It takes me about ten minutes to drive to the pool hall Ms. Lewis had mentioned. I'm not surprised that this is where Tommy likes to spend his time. The Corner Pocket is a popular hangout for the local Crips. At any given time, there are always several of them hanging around. I've spent many nights outside, waiting for one member or another. Tonight I won't be waiting. I'll be going inside.

Since I've dealt with a lot of these guys before it will be no secret exactly who I am, so I decide to work with that. I walk right inside and feel the eyes of several people land on me the second I do. The conversations dull to a quiet hum and I hear the words "pig" and "fuckin' cop" coming from all directions.

Spotting Tommy off in the corner, jaw clenched and eyes boring a hole into me, I head in his direction. "Tommy Lewis?"

He stands up taller, his body practically vibrating with agitation. "Who the fuck wants to know, pig?"

This kid isn't going to talk to me here. I knew that already. Taking another step forward, I flash my badge at him. "My name is Sergeant Lawson. I'm here about your Mom."

I watch the blood drain from his face, and suddenly he loses all appearance of a thug and looks like just a scared little boy. I almost feel bad for lying to him — but not really.

"Is she okay?" he asks, his voice sounding a whole lot less tough than it did just a second ago.

"I'm afraid not, Mr. Lewis. I'm going to need you to come with me."

He doesn't argue. Turning, he leans his pool cue up against the wall and mumbles something to the guys he was playing with. All eyes are on us as I walk out of the pool hall, Tommy close on my heels.

We get to my unmarked cruiser and I open the back door for him to climb inside. I can see the tears now forming in his eyes as he ducks his head to get in. Rounding the vehicle, I jump into the driver's seat but don't start the car. Placing my hands on the steering wheel, I stare straight ahead.

"What's going on? What happened to my Mom?"

I don't move. Glancing up into the rear view mirror, I see Tommy sitting back there, behind the glass partition. "Your mother's fine, Tommy."

He sits forward, his face confused and angry. "What? You said something happened to my Mom! What the fuck is going on? You stupid fuckin' pig. Let me the fuck out of this fuckin' pig wagon." His hands scrabble at the door handle, desperately trying to open it, but the door is locked and can't be unlocked from back there. I sit silently while he bangs on the door in frustration and turns his hate filled eyes to me. "You can't hold me here. I know my fuckin' rights."

"Where's Derrick Monroe?"

He freezes, his eyes locked on mine through the mirror. "What?"

"I said where is Derrick Monroe."

His eyes narrow and he glares at me with immeasurable hatred. "Fuck you."

I sigh and decide to try a different tactic. "You know...you really hurt Gabby today. She was in tears when I talked to her." He stops glaring and his face turns sad. "She loves you, ya know."

Tommy says nothing but I can almost see the war he has raging inside his head. I stay silent, letting it play out. Finally he looks up at me, his eyes meeting mine in the mirror once more. "They'll kill me."

47

I shake my head. "They'll never know it was you, Tommy."

He shakes his head. "They'll know. They always know."

I turn my body and face him through the barrier. "Is Derrick alive, Tommy?"

His jaw hardens and slowly he nods his head. "Barely."

Hope fills me. There's still time. "Will you take me to him?" Tommy nods once more and I face forward again, starting up my cruiser. "Where am I going, Tommy?"

Tommy sits up tall in his seat and rattles off the address. I put the car in drive and pull away from the curb, anxious to get to Derrick before it's too late.

Gabby

After Daniel leaves my house, I sit on my couch and stew. I'm pissed at myself, not only for allowing myself to be distracted from my search for Derrick by a sexy cop, but also for allowing Daniel to touch me the way he did only to blow me off afterwards and just walk out the door.

I'm not an idiot. I know why he did what he did. I respect him for having more self-control than I do and for doing what was best for me and my brother. Even knowing all that, the rejection still stings a little.

Forcing my thoughts back to my brother, I think back to Tommy's behaviour at the coffee shop. In hindsight and knowing Tommy for as long as I have, I realize that he really was just putting on a show. Hurting me had hurt him.

And if hurting me hurt him, I know that hurting Derrick would just about kill him. He might not know where Derrick is, but he knows more than I do, which at this point is absolutely nothing.

Daniel had said that he was going to Tommy's house. My mind had been a little distracted at the time but I have no doubt that Tommy will not be home. He hates his house, only going there to shower and sometimes to sleep if there is nowhere else to go. If this is just a regular night for him, he'll be at The Corner Pocket.

Nodding my head, I jump up from the couch and grab my seldom-used car keys. Mom had left her car here when she moved out west for me to use whenever I wanted. I rarely use it though, opting instead to walk or take a taxi. Parking in this city is ridiculous.

Heading for the garage, I hit the button on the wall and open the car door as the garage door rattles open. Sticking the key into the ignition, I give it a twist and listen to the car come to life. The little Kia Rio hasn't been started since I took it out to visit a friend in the suburbs three weeks ago.

I pull out of the driveway and make my way to the pool hall, praying that Tommy will be there. I don't know if I can go through another sleepless night, wondering if my brother is okay. The drive only takes a few minutes, and on the way I plan out exactly what I am going to say to him. I know his buddies will be around and that he'll likely be a dick at first, but this time I'll be prepared. I will yank him out of there by the ear if I have to.

Pulling up to the curb, I make my best attempt to parallel park the Rio. I only having to pull out and back in again four times. That's a new record for me. I'm just reaching for the handle when I see Daniel come walking out of the pool hall, Tommy close on his heels, his face looking sad.

I watch as Daniel opens the back door of an unmarked

cruiser and walks around to the driver's side. *Where are they going? Does Tommy know where Derrick is?* I consider getting out and approaching the car but I'm worried that I'll be interfering with whatever Daniel is doing to get Tommy to co-operate. Besides, my car is parked several cars behind them. I'd never make it to them before they pull away.

But they don't pull away. From where I sit, I can make out the shadows of both men, and neither seem to be moving much. Suddenly, the shadow in the back starts jerking around, arms flailing and it almost looks like he's hitting the windows but I can't be sure. What the hell is going on?

I reach across the seat and rummage through my purse without taking my eyes off the shadows in that car. When I finally locate my phone, I pull it out and get ready to dial Daniel's cell phone. I want to let him know that I'm here.

I just dial the last number when the Tommy's shadow sits up straight and the car pulls away from the curb. Daniel's phone rings four times before his voice mail picks up.

"Daniel? It's Gabby." I put my car in drive and pull out onto the street, following the unmarked car. "Um…I went to The Corner Pocket to see if I could find Tommy, and saw you and him getting into your car. Did he tell you where Derrick is? Anyways, I'm right behind you. Call me back."

Pressing the end button, I toss the phone on the seat beside me and do my best to keep up with the speeding car.

Daniel

I see Gabby's number ringing through on the screen and silence the ringer. Tommy is behind me, finally telling me everything and I'm not about to interrupt him when I'm so close to finding Derrick.

"So this kid at school started selling us weed, ya know? And me and Derrick, we thought he was a cool kid, and we liked his supply, so we started hanging out with him after school and shit." I keep my eyes on the road, but every now and then look back to where Tommy sits, talking with his head back on the seat, eyes on the ceiling.

"Turns out, this kid is a Crip. We start hanging out with a bunch of them at different spots. We even make a few friends. Derrick and I both started selling weed for them. Just small time shit, ya know? Dime bags to buddies from high school mostly." He shakes his head. "After a while, they started teaching us some shit about how they work. Invited us both to parties. We spent a lot of time high, man. And the ladies …" He smirks and shakes his head. "The ladies were everywhere, ya know? Man, we were gettin' laid almost every night."

"Who was taking you to these parties?"

Tommy leans forward and his eyes meet mine in the rear-view mirror. "Fuck that, man. I'll take you to Derrick. I'll even tell you his story, but I'm no narc. You hear that?" I nod, knowing that he might not have much choice before this is all done. Giving up the gang may be the only way the cops can offer him protection.

Tommy sits back in his seat. "Anyway, all of the sudden the other guys were going to parties and we weren't invited. It was bullshit, man. Pissed us both off. We were told those parties were for members only. Finally, one of them asks us if we want to become members ourselves. Derrick and I both said yes. We'd have been crazy not to. The weed and women alone made the initiation worth it."

I look back at him through the mirror. "What was the initiation?"

He smirks. "No way, man. Not tellin' you that shit either. I *will* say that we had to do something specific. Something illegal. Once that was done, we were in — full-fledged Crips."

"So what happened?"

Tommy shakes his head. "Derrick started talkin' to some bitch online. She lives in the country somewhere on some fuckin' horse farm. He took her out a few times. Stupid fucker told me that she was the one. You imagine? Dude is nineteen years old and he thinks he found the *one*?"

I take the next exit, our destination only a few blocks away.

"Anyway, Derrick goes up to the head guy, ya know? Not gonna tell ya more than I need to, but basically he tells him he wants out. Buddy tells him it ain't that easy. Derrick says he don't fuckin' care. He's movin' away and wants to go to college with this bitch and he'll do what he needs to do." Tommy shakes his head and sniffs, trying to look unaffected by his own story. "Buddy tells him the only way he'll let Derrick out is to jump him out."

I know exactly what that means. You don't work on the Street Crimes Unit and not know what a jump out is. Basically, if a gang member wants out and the gang is willing to let him go without fear of him turning on them and trading their secrets, they'll do a jump out. It's where every member of the gang takes turns beating the shit out of the member. If he lives, he's out. Free from the gang.

"Is Derrick alive, Tommy?"

He nods solemnly. "Barely." I pull into the driveway of the address he gave me and look up at the large abandoned warehouse. This building had been on police radar for a while for being a hub for gang activity. Tommy directs me towards a rear entrance and keeps talking.

"Those fuckers kicked the shit out of him, man. Even I had to take my turn or I'd have looked like a pussy." His breath wavers a little. "When they were done, everyone went their separate ways but Derrick didn't get up. He was bleeding like crazy and I could tell that some of his bones were broken."

"Why didn't you take him to the hospital?"

"They were watching me, man. The boss though, he liked Derrick, and he let me pull him off into one of the offices and said if I could nurse him back to health, he was free to go." I pull to a stop and look back to see Tommy shake his head sadly. "It's not good, man."

"Take me to him."

Getting out of the car, I let Tommy out of the back and he leads me inside the building, moving quietly for fear that someone is around. The place seems deserted. Finally, we round a corner and there he is.

Laying on a pile of dirty rags is a barely recognizable Derrick. His face is black and blue and swollen. One look at him tells me that he has fractures to his face and right arm, and God knows where else. I rush to him, squatting down beside his broken form and feel for a pulse. It's weak, but it's there.

I pull out my phone, ready to call 911 when I hear a loud click from behind. Both Tommy and I spin around, and the blood drains from my face.

The first thing I see is the gun, cocked and ready. And then I see where it's pointed. Gabby's terrified face is white as a sheet and covered in silent tears as the gun presses hard against her temple. The shaking and angry man holding the gun clutches Gabby to his body with a forearm across her throat.

"I knew you were a fuckin' rat, Tommy," he spits. "Fuckin' piece of shit."

Gabby

I keep my eyes pinned on Daniel, my body shaking with fear. Everything happened so fast that I didn't see this guy's face. I pulled up behind Daniel's car and walked inside, listening for the sounds of their voices in the empty warehouse.

I heard the faint echo of footsteps off to the right and moved in that direction. I didn't make it more than three steps before a strong arm wrapped around my neck and a gun is stabbed into my cheek. "Don't fucking scream, bitch."

The truth is, when he grabbed me I lost all of the air in

my lungs. I couldn't have screamed if I wanted to. With wide eyes I stare at the gun that is being held only inches from my eye. "Keep your mouth shut and do what I say," he orders and starts walking, my body propelled along in front of his as he moves silently towards the sounds I'd been following a few seconds ago.

We round a corner and my body sags in relief when I see Daniel. The strange man behind me pulls the gun away from my face and uses his thumb to cock the hammer before pressing the muzzle to my temple.

Both Tommy and Daniel spin around, Daniel's hand moving towards his hip. "I knew you were a fuckin' rat, Tommy," the man spits. "Fuckin' piece of shit."

Tears fill my eyes as I stare at Daniel who stands frozen in front of us, eyes locked on me, his jaw set. I watch as Tommy throws out his arms.

"Tooth, man," he pleads. "You know I'd never rat. I just want Derrick to get some help, brother. He's my best friend." One of his hands drop while he's talking and points at a pile of rags in the corner.

"Fuck you," Tooth snarls. "You brought a fuckin' cop to a fuckin' Crip joint and likely told him all kinds of shit. Then ya got this bitch creepin' through the goddamn building."

I hear them talking, but I don't know what they're saying. My body trembles and my head screams as I stare at that rumpled pile of rags. Only it's not rags. It's my brother. My breath catches in my chest and I forget all about the gun pressed against my head. Attempting to shrug him off, I let out an anguished cry. "Derrick!"

He doesn't move. I try to pull free once more and Tooth yanks me back, screaming into my ear. "Don't move you crazy fuckin' bitch!" He presses the gun even harder to my head, grinding it into my skull. "I'm gonna blow your fuckin' brains all over this fucking room!"

I feel his hand move and my eyes lift to Daniel's, an apology on my lips. Just then, Tommy lurches forward. "No! Tooth! Don't—"

The sound of the gun going off so close to my face nearly deafens me, my head fills with a loud ringing as I stare in horror at Tommy. He clutches his chest, his mouth open in surprise as the blood stain on his shirt grows bigger right before my eyes. His mouth makes no sound as he drops to his knees.

I know I'm screaming, but I can't hear my own voice over the high-pitched ringing in my head. When Tommy slumps forward and lands face first on the floor, I know deep down that he's dead. My eyes move to Daniel.

Like a fearless warrior, he stands proudly in front of my brother, protecting his body with his own, his arm raised as he holds his gun firmly in his hand. Instantly, my mind clears and I scramble to come up with some sort of plan. We can't die like this.

"I said drop it, pig!"

Daniel's voice is strong and fearless, his gun held steady. "Let the girl go. She was just trying to find her brother."

Tooth's body tenses behind mine and he mutters a soft, "Fuck it."

Before I know what's happening, he pulls the gun away from my temple and points it right at Daniel. He pulls the trigger before I can react and I watch in horror as Daniel crumples to the ground.

"No!" I scream, struggling to free myself from his hold. "Daniel!" Daniel doesn't move. Suddenly, I'm flying across the room, my body landing on top of my brother's in the corner. He doesn't even open his eyes as I look down at his broken body.

"You wanted to find your fuckin' pussy ass brother so bad, bitch? Well there he is. Now you can both go to hell!" He raises the gun and time seems to stop as I watch his finger slide over the trigger. I drape my body over Derrick's and squeeze my eyes closed.

The gunshot rings through the warehouse and my body jerks in surprise and tenses, waiting for the bullet to hit me. Something drops to the floor and I lift my head, wondering what the hell is going on.

Tooth lays crumpled just a foot away, a disgusting looking hole drilled right through his forehead. My heart pounds as I lift my eyes and see Daniel slump to the floor clutching his arm. He's out of breath when he looks up at me and asks, "You okay, baby?"

Daniel

I shrug my shirt back on and slide off the hospital bed. After a quick examination that the Chief had insisted on, the doctor cleaned my wound and declared that it was a clean shot, the bullet going in one side of my arm and out the other. Six stitches and a bandage later, and I'm free to go.

I was lucky, and I know that. I was definitely luckier than poor Tommy Lewis. The Chief had confirmed what I already knew. The shot Tommy had taken in the chest had been fatal. He had died within seconds. The Chief left just a few minutes ago to deliver the news to Ms. Lewis himself. I didn't envy him.

After buttoning my shirt, I move through the emergency room and head straight for the elevator. Gabby is on the third floor, waiting for her brother to get out of surgery. They still weren't sure if he was going to make it. He'd lost a lot of blood and there had been a lot of internal damage done in the beatings. Infection had set in from just laying on the floor, in a heap for days.

When the elevator door opens, I turn to the left and there she is. Her hair is a mess and her makeup is smudged all over her face. I've never seen a more beautiful sight in all my life. When she sees me, she doesn't hesitate. She covers the distance between us at a run and slams into my chest, her arms wrapping themselves tightly around my waist.

"Oh, Daniel. I'm so glad you're okay."

I chuckle softly and hug her tight, pressing my lips into the top of her hair. "I'm fine, baby. Just a few stitches." We hold each other in silence, our bodies slowly rocking from side to side. "Any news on Derrick yet?"

She pulls her cheek from my chest and looks up at me, her face sad as she shakes her head. I give her a reassuring squeeze. "Have faith, babe. If Derrick is anything like his sister, he's a tough son of a bitch and will be just fine."

A small smile appears on her face and she shakes her head. "He's more like me than he'll ever admit."

I grin down at her, glad to see she still has a sense of humour. Taking her hand, I guide her to the waiting room chairs and pull her down beside me. Wrapping my arm around her shoulders, I pull her body against mine and whisper, "Sleep, babe."

She shakes her head, not looking up from where it rests on my shoulder. "I can't," she whispers back.

"You can," I say. "I'm not going anywhere. I'll wake you if the doctor comes in."

She sits up, unable to hide her surprise. "You're staying?"

I frown. "Of course I'm staying."

Her sigh is heavy and her shoulders droop. "I can't ask you to do that, Daniel. You have your own life to live.

You've done so much for me already —"

Gripping her chin between my thumb and forefinger, I tilt her face so she can't avoid my eyes. "I said I'm not going anywhere." She looks confused so I decide to make it a little clearer for her. "Gabby...I've known you for two days. That's it. Two." She frowns, but I keep going. "And in that time you've done some shit that deserves a serious spanking." Her eyes widen and she sits up in her chair. "But even though it's only been two days, I couldn't imagine leaving you here alone. The thought of being away from you at all feels wrong."

Her eyes search mine, tears threatening to spill from their blue depths. And then she smiles. Her smile lights up her whole face. It also lights up a place inside of me that I didn't even know had been dark.

Pulling her towards me, I cover her lips with my own and show her just how much she's grown to mean to me. Her lips move against mine, her hands clutching my shirt. When I finally pull away, her cheeks are flushed and her lips are swollen.

A thought suddenly occurs to me. "Hey, did you know that Derrick has a girlfriend?"

She jerks and her brows drop low over her eyes. "What?"

Gabby

Seven hours and an achy back later, the doctor finally comes to find me in the waiting room. "Miss Monroe?"

I bolt upright in my chair, my heart in my throat. "Yes?"

"Miss Monroe, I'm Dr. Connolly. I've been operating on your brother all night." I stare at him, afraid to even blink while I wait for him to finally tell me if Derrick is going to be okay. "It was touch and go there for a while. Your brother had a lot of internal injuries and a skull fracture. His lung was punctured by a broken rib and he lost a lot of blood."

Daniel reaches over and grabs my hand, giving it a squeeze. I just nod at the doctor and wait for him to continue.

"The good news is I think we got it all. He has a lot of stitches, both inside and out. He has a lot of broken bones that will need to heal and he will likely need another blood transfusion before the end of the night." He stuffs his hands into the deep pockets of his lab coat. "The bad news is there was a lot of bleeding in his brain. He had a skull fracture that did some damage to the tissue there. We won't know how much until your brother wakes up."

I can't speak. Fear wraps its cold hand around my throat and squeezes with all its might. "When will that be?" Daniel asks.

"I don't know. Derrick has been through a major trauma. We've done what we can surgically. The rest is up to him."

I manage to find my voice and squeak out a quiet, "Can we see him?"

The doctor looks to Daniel and then to me. "Family only, I'm afraid. If you'd like to sit with him though, I can take you to him."

I look to Daniel who places a tender kiss on my forehead and gives me a gentle shove. "Go. I'll be right here if you need me."

It's at that moment that I realize that nobody has ever said that to me. Nobody has ever been there when I needed them. I have been there for myself. And for Derrick, and Tommy. My mother had never been capable of being there for anyone but herself and after Gunner left, I stopped counting on people. Standing up on my tiptoes, I press my lips against Daniel's, fighting back the emotion that his words caused.

"Thank you," I whisper, then turn and follow the doctor

through a set of heavy doors and down a long, brightly lit hallway.

He leads me to a room that has the curtains drawn and the lights turned low. The only bed in the room holds my baby brother. I nod at the doctor and approach the bed, taking Derrick's hand in my own. He almost looks better than he did the last time I saw him. The blood has been cleaned from his skin and he has more colour than he did before, despite the white bandages that cover large areas of his body.

I lean forward and place a kiss on the only small area of his forehead that isn't covered in gauze. "Get better, Derrick," I whisper.

**

Two days pass before Derrick finally wakes up. I don't leave his side the entire time. Daniel has been wonderful through it all, making sure that I have everything I need. He feeds me and brings me clean clothes, and whenever I need a hug he's always in the waiting room.

On the second day, I'm sitting in my chair reading an article from Cosmo out loud, secretly wondering if I annoy Derrick enough will he wake up and tell me to keep my mouth shut. I'm just getting to the good part. Sex tip number seventeen is especially descriptive and makes me wonder if I should start stretching before I attempt it.

I glance up from my magazine and my heart stops. Derrick is staring at me, a small smile on his face. I toss the magazine aside and move to his side in a flash. "You'll need to stretch first," he croaks, his voice raspy and muted from days of not being used.

"Derrick," I gasp. "Oh, thank God! I was so scared. How are you feeling?"

"Thirsty," he croaks.

I reach over his head and press the button to summon a

nurse. "The nurse will get you something. God, Derrick. When you get better, I'm gonna kick your ass!"

He smiles a little and stares at me, his eyes tired and filled with pain. "I look forward to it, Gabby."

**

A couple of days later, I'm helping Derrick eat some soup when I can't hold it in anymore. I continue offering him spoonfuls of the hot broth while I ask the question I just can't figure out. "Why did you join that gang, Derrick?"

He waves away the spoon with a weak hand and shakes his head. "I don't know really. They seemed like cool guys. I guess Tommy and I both just wanted to fit in." He looks off towards the window and shakes his head. "Pretty stupid, huh?"

I say nothing because he's right. It was pretty stupid, but I'm not going to make him feel worse than he already does. "Tommy saved me you know." Derrick looks at me and his eyes grow wet. "That Tooth guy would have shot me if Tommy hadn't tried to stop him."

He reaches up and dashes away an escaped tear and snorts. "Tommy loved you, Gabby."

I look at him and smile. "He did?"

He nods and smiles back. "Yep. Said you had the nicest rack he'd ever seen."

I laugh and shake my head. "Whatever. I loved him too. Tommy was a good kid. I'll miss him."

He opens his mouth just as a knock sounds on the door. Standing in the doorway, looking completely out of place, is Gunner. Derrick frowns in confusion, not knowing who Gunner is.

"Gunner," I say, standing from my chair beside Derrick's bed. "What are you doing here?" I hadn't talked to Gunner since the other day when he'd agreed to help me find my brother. It had been an awkward conversation at best, but I know that deep down Gunner cares about both of us. He just didn't know how to fight for us. We'll never have a loving daddy-daughter relationship, but I'd like to think that maybe we can all get to know each other now. I suddenly feel bad. After everything that had happened I had forgotten to call Gunner.

"Daniel called me," he replies from the door. "I just wanted to check in, see how you both are doing."

"Gabby?" Derrick asks, his face scrunched up in confusion.

My heart pounds as I prepare to make an introduction that should never have to be made. Especially not to a grown man who grew up without a father. "Derrick, meet Gunner Monroe." Derrick's wide eyes swing from me to Gunner. "Your father."

Daniel

I'm not surprised to see Travis come sauntering into the waiting room while Gunner is back visiting with Gabby and Derrick. He gives me a nod and takes the seat beside me. We sit in silence for a few minutes before he finally speaks.

"Your sister's pissed at you," he drawls.

I snap my head around and look at him, surprised. Then it dawns on me. I haven't called Laynie since all this shit went down, and I missed my birthday. Of course I had seen that she'd called me a few times, but I'd been sitting in a packed waiting room each time and always forgot to call her back. Dropping my head back against the wall behind me, I sigh. "How pissed?"

He chuckles. "Pretty pissed."

"Shit." We're silent for a few more seconds, me trying

to find a way to make it up to my sister. "I could come over for dinner on the weekend?"

Travis raises his brow. "I look like a fuckin' caterer to you? Call your fuckin' sister, man."

Just then Gabby and Gunner come through the heavy doors separating the hospital rooms from the waiting area. I watch silently as Gabby smiles at him and looks uncertain, then shoots her hand out for a handshake.

Gunner grins and shakes her hand, his eyes showing his happiness. As one, Travis and Gunner give us a farewell nod as they move toward the exit. I'm just pulling Gabby in for a hug when Travis calls from the door, "You know Laynie will want you to bring her."

I roll my eyes and nod my head, watching as he finally leaves. Gabby looks up and tilts her head to the side. "Who's Laynie?"

**

That weekend things finally seem to settle down. Derrick had been moved from intensive care and was bouncing off the walls in a ward room on the fourth floor, more than ready to go home. From the sounds of things, he'll be released tomorrow.

Gabby and I have been spending a lot of time together, though I do have to return to work after next week. Apparently, a bullet in the arm only justifies two weeks off. Gabby is going back to work on Monday.

After much apologizing, and only a little grovelling, Laynie has finally forgiven me. Gabby and I had just left her place after stuffing ourselves with delicious food and good wine. Introducing Gabby to my sister felt completely natural. The two ladies had hit it off right away.

Halfway through the dinner, they started planning a girl's night and Travis had looked just as worried as I felt. Gabby and Laynie together, combined with a mixture of alcohol and loud music, was a recipe for disaster if you ask me.

Watching Travis and my sister tonight had been a surprise. When I'd first discovered they were a couple, I instantly disapproved of him, terrified what a relationship with him could mean for my blind sister. But seeing her tonight, the way she smiled and the way Travis dotes on her, set my mind at ease. My sister was finally happy, and I had Travis to thank for that.

Pulling up to Gabby's house, I take the key from the ignition and step out of the car. I walk around to the passenger side, open the door and help Gabby out of the vehicle. Taking her hand, we walk towards the house and up the front steps to the door. Once inside, Gabby tosses her keys on the small table in the foyer and walks towards the kitchen.

"Want a beer?" she calls back over her shoulder.

"Please," I reply, moving straight for the couch.

She enters the room and flops down beside me, handing over my opened bottle. Turning her body towards mine, she takes a swig of her own beer and smiles. "Your sister is amazing."

I nod and smile. "She is. Laynie is one of a kind."

She takes another swig. "You know, it's funny. I wouldn't picture them together. Laynie and Travis? But seeing them tonight, they just…fit…ya know?"

I nod my head. "I didn't. But I'm starting to."

We both fall silent and stare off in opposite directions, each lost in our own thoughts. I look over at her and catch her looking at me with a soft smile on her face. I grin. "What?"

She shakes her head. "You're just a really good guy." Her cheeks flush and I watch as the pink continues from her cheeks all the way down her neck and spreads across her chest. "I don't know what I would have done if you hadn't come along when I was storming out of the police station that day."

I smile back at her and reach out to take her hand. "Well, Frank would probably still have a job."

Her eyes widen and she laughs. "He got fired?" I nod, grinning at the joy she seems to feel from this news. "Well good! He was a dick."

I throw my head back and laugh. She's right. He was a dick. Suddenly, Gabby's face is inches from mine and has lost all traces of laughter. My smile fades as I stare into her eyes.

"I want to finish what we started, Daniel."

I don't make her wait. Reaching out, I wrap my hand around the back of her head and pull her lips to mine with an urgency that makes my heart pound. I revel in the feel of her lips, knowing that this time I don't have to stop. But I can't do it here. Not on the couch.

Pulling her up with me, I stand up, scooping her into my arms like a bride on her wedding day. "Bedroom," I rasp.

She points to the stairway and I all but run up them, anxious to finally make this woman mine. Gabby directs me down the hall to a room on the right. The room is black and red and covered in silks and satins but I don't have time to admire it.

Setting her on the bed, I crawl onto it and cover her body with mine. As I explore her lips with my own, I can feel the unsteady thump of her heart beating against my chest. Sitting up on my knees, I stare down at her as I peel off my shirt. She watches my every movement, and when I'm done, she returns the favour.

Whisking her dress up and over her head, she tosses it to the floor. Her large, creamy breasts all but spill out of the black lace bra she's wearing. Leaning down, I trace the seam of her bra with my tongue, enjoying the little hitch I hear in her breathing, confirming to me that she likes what I'm doing.

With one finger, I pull down the cup on one side and expose her large dusky nipple. I keep my eyes locked on hers as I dip my head and wrap my lips around it, swirling the peak with my tongue. I watch as her lips part and her head falls back, a soft moan escaping her throat.

Placing tender kisses on the peak of each breast I travel even lower, showering her with soft, wet kisses in a line down her belly. When I reach the hem of her matching panties, she whimpers softly. Running my finger over her mound, I feel her arousal soaking through the lacy material. My eyes burn into hers as I lower my face and blow my hot breath over her clit.

Her hands come down, clamping onto the sides of my face, her eyes sparking with fire. "Don't tease me, Daniel. Any other time, that would be okay. This isn't that time."

"You can't rush perfection, baby."

She glares down at me and I just wink as I slide her panties down her legs and toss them over the side of the bed. Spreading her legs wide, I take in the sight of her glistening pink pussy and look up at her with a grin. "Hold on, baby."

Her reply comes out as little more than a squeak when I lower my head and suck her already swollen clit deep into my mouth. Her hands sink into my hair and I feel her hips buck as I release her clit and flick it back and forth with my flattened tongue. The sounds of her moans fill the room.

Her moans and gasps grow louder and faster and I know that she's close. That's good, because after the last few days, so am I. Pulling away, I slide off my pants and pull out a condom, ripping the wrapper open with my teeth before sliding it on.

Still holding her legs wide, I settle myself on my knees, my cock pressed against her entrance and trail it up and down collecting her wetness. When I graze her clit with the tip, she gasps and shudders, a loud curse escaping her swollen lips.

Holding my cock in my hands, I position it at her entrance and we both watch, heads tilted down as I push my way inside of her, rocking in and out until I've buried my length as far as I can go. Beads of sweat form on my brow and Gabby's cheeks flame a blotchy red as she stares at me, her mouth open and panting.

Slowly I roll my hips, watching her take my cock. Pressing my thumb against her clit, I move faster with each thrust, making sure each time I hit the end a little harder than the last. Our combined cries fill the room and I watch in awe as Gabby reaches down between us and touches where we're connected.

Her pussy clenches tighter until I feel like I'm in a vice—a warm, wet, silky vice. Heat builds low in my spine and I can feel my orgasm coming. Thrusting harder, I roll my thumb in circles on her swollen clit, desperate to take her with me when I cum.

Her body starts to tremble and her low moans turn to a loud keening that is all but drowned out by the sounds of my own pleasure as we both ride the wave of our orgasm, our hips grinding desperately into each other.

I slow my rolling hips and lean down, covering her mouth with my own. Our kiss is slow, and wet and sweaty as we both try to catch our breath. I pull my head back and swipe the hair from her face, pressing a kiss to the tip of her nose.

Pulling out of her heat, I rise from the bed and move to what I can see is an adjoining bathroom. After I dispose of the condom, I crawl back into bed, pulling Gabby into my arms. Tilting her face towards mine, I press my lips to hers once more, not wanting to end our kiss. Softly our lips explore, tasting and sipping from one another as our heartbeats return to normal.

The sudden ringing of the phone startles us both. Turning to the side, Gabby sees the number flash across the screen and turns to me with wide eyes. "It's my mother… finally."

We hadn't talked much about Gabby's mother but I noticed that she hadn't even called through all of this though I know Gabby had made several calls to her, all of which went to voicemail.

"Let it go to voicemail," she says with a grin, her lips descending on mine once more.

Kings of Acknowledgements Korruption

To Tammie Smith & Blue Remy – You put together an amazing anthology and event, full of authors that I now consider friends. Thank you for the time and effort you put into it. This story would never have been written (or at least not this soon) if you had not had the desire to do OAMC.

To Christina DeRoche – Thank you for an amazing brainstorming session over birthday drinks at the comedy club. Your ideas were fantastic and I love that you love the Kings as much as I do.

To Jacqueline M Sinclair – Your beta reading was spot on as usual. I love your face.

To Amanda DiPierro – You are my favorite pimp, and don't ever forget it. I could never write without your help in all other areas of my promotion!

To Nicole Lloyd – My fastest beta reader, and other favorite pimp. Your face is another one I love ;)

To Johnna Siebert – Thank you for working so hard to get your authors out there. We couldn't do it without you!

To Tracey Jackson – Your opinions mean the world to me, and your formatting saves me every time. Thank you!!!

To Robin at Wicked By Design – Another beautiful cover, and many more to come ;) I may be your biggest fan.

To April at ACS Media – Thank you for the thorough editing, and honest critiquing. Editors like you are so hard to find, and you make me look good ;) I can't praise you enough.

To The Bloggers – There are way too many blogs to name them all, but you know who you are. If you've ever shared, posted or commented on my work, THANK YOU a million times over. Without you, nobody would have even heard of the Kings of Korruption.

To My Readers – Your support blows me away. I will never be able to express how much you all mean to me. Love each and every one of you.

About Geri

Geri Glenn is the author of Kings of Korruption MC Series and a co-author of Hybrids.

Geri lives in beautiful New Brunswick, Canada. She is an army wife, the mother of two gorgeous, but slightly crazy little girls, and just recently was fortunate enough to quit her day job to stay home and do what she loves most – write!

Geri has been as avid reader for as long as she can remember. When she isn't writing or adulting in some other fashion, she can usually be found curled up in a comfy chair, reading on her iPad both day and night. Geri is an incurable night owl, and it's not uncommon for her to still be awake, reading at 4 am, just because she finds it hard to put the book down.

Geri loves all genres of fiction, but her passion is anything romantic or terrifying; basically, anything that can get her heart pumping. This passion has bled out onto her laptop and became the Kings of Korruption.

Writing that first book in the series has knocked off the #1 thing on Geri's bucket list, and publishing it has been an absolute dream come true. She hopes you love the Kings as much as she does.

Stalk her!

♛ Facebook: https://www.facebook.com/geriglennauthor
♛ Twitter: https://twitter.com/authorgeriglenn
♛ Instagram: https://instagram.com/authorgeriglenn/
♛ Website: http://geriglenn.com/
♛ Amazon: http://goo.gl/BlnP6R
♛ Goodreads: https://goo.gl/BHK4h0